Mystery Cat and the Chocolate Trap

by Susan Saunders
Illustrated by Eileen Christelow

A Bantam Skylark Book
Toronto · New York · London · Sydney · Auckland

RL 3, 008–011

MYSTERY CAT AND THE CHOCOLATE TRAP
A Bantam Skylark Book/July 1986

Skylark Books is a registered trademark of Bantam Books, Inc.
Registered in U.S. Patent and Trademark Office and elsewhere.

Mystery Cat is a trademark of Cloverdale Press Inc.

Produced by Cloverdale Press Inc.

ISBN 0-553-15415-X

Published simultaneously in the United States and Canada

Bantam Books are published by Bantam Books, Inc. Its trademark, consisting of the
words "Bantam Books" and the portrayal of a rooster, is Registered in U.S. Patent
and Trademark Office and in other countries. Marca Registrada. Bantam Books,
Inc., 666 Fifth Avenue, New York, New York 10103.

PRINTED IN THE UNITED STATES OF AMERICA

CW   0 9 8 7 6 5 4 3 2 1

Chapter One

It wasn't the first time Mystery Cat had disappeared. But Kelly Ann McCoy couldn't help worrying. The big gray cat hadn't shown up at her house for three days. And her best friend, Hillary Barnett, hadn't seen him, either. What if something had happened to him? Was anyone feeding him? Had he gotten into trouble again?

Mystery Cat had strolled into Kelly Ann's life just before school was out for the summer. That he had a history was obvious by his torn ear and crooked tail. But he wore no collar, he was very dirty, and he had the hungry look of an animal who hadn't had a square meal in months. Kelly Ann's father was sure he was a stray.

Right away the cat let the McCoys' chicken-hearted dog, Samantha, know he was no one to trifle with. Then he hung around the yard, hoping for a handout. Kelly Ann felt sorry for the scruffy animal. He needed someone to take care of him.

Mr. McCoy was a small contractor. He added rooms onto houses, reroofed and reshingled them, and built garages. But business had been slow recently. Even though Mrs. McCoy worked part-time, a family of five—Kelly Ann had seven-year-old twin brothers—plus Samantha, was expensive. Another pet was exactly what the McCoys *didn't* need.

But Kelly Ann promised to pay for the gray cat's food out of her baby-sitting money. She named him Lancelot, because she had just been reading about King Arthur's bravest knight.

At about the same time, a battle-scarred gray cat turned up at the Barnetts' big new house on the other side of Windsor's Main Street. He staged a hit-and-run attack on a bag of meat Mrs. Barnett had just brought home from the butcher shop. Hillary Barnett rode up on her bike in time to see the cat streak away with a string of specially ground veal-and-pork sausages.

Hillary liked his style, and since she didn't have a pet, she decided to keep the cat. Hillary's mother couldn't understand why her daughter would want such a disreputable-looking animal. But Hillary's lawyer father admired the cat's spunkiness. So the cat stayed. Hillary named him Frank—short for Frankfurter—in honor of their first meeting.

For several weeks, Frank spent part of the night and most of the morning at Hillary's. And Lancelot spent the afternoon and most of the evening at Kelly Ann's. If both girls hadn't gone to the Windsor Police Station on the same day—one to report Lancelot missing, the other to report Frank found—they probably never would have learned the truth: *Frank and Lancelot were one and the same cat.*

The girls found out some other things, too. Several of the police officers had known the tough old stray with a notched ear for a long time. They called him Mystery Cat—M.C. for short, because he had a way of mysteriously turning up wherever the action was: traffic jams, fires, arrests, even a bank robbery.

"You may as well share him," they advised the two girls, "because nobody *owns* that cat, but nobody."

So Hillary and Kelly Ann agreed to share their pet. And they soon shared a friendship as well.

M.C. divided his time between the McCoys and the Barnetts. It wasn't long before he lived up to his name and got the girls involved in a full-fledged mystery that had to do with a pair of phony ten-dollar bills, as well as a pair of very real counterfeiters.

With help from M.C., the mystery was solved. Then Hillary went off to camp in Maine, and Kelly Ann settled into her summer. There were the twins to keep an eye on, baby-sitting jobs, baseball games and picnics and swimming in the park. Of course, there were lots of trips to the library, too, since Kelly Ann loved to read.

M.C. continued his rounds, with Hillary's parents feeding him in the morning and Kelly Ann feeding him in the evening. Now Hillary was back—but M.C. was gone!

All Hillary would say when she and Kelly Ann talked about it was: "I'm sure he's okay. That cat has at least *ninety-nine* lives." But Kelly Ann knew Hillary was beginning to worry, too.

Both girls had called the Windsor animal shelter. What else could they do? Sometimes people advertised for lost pets in the newspaper. But how would you describe M.C.? Kelly Ann sat down at the kitchen table and wrote in her notebook: "LOST: Gray adult male cat, age unknown. Piece missing from left ear. Small kink near end of tail. Answers to. . ." What *did* M.C. answer to?

Kelly Ann shook her head and started writing again: "Answers when he wants to. Can be recognized by his *very* mysterious manner."

Kelly Ann was so deep in thought that her younger brothers had to call her twice before she heard them.

"Kelly Ann!" Andrew and Michael, the twins, were playing in the backyard. "It's M.C.!"

Kelly Ann was out the door in a flash. There M.C. was, all right, looking smug. Kelly Ann was so glad to see him she thought for a minute she was going to cry. Instead she scolded:

4

"M.C., you bad cat! Where have you been?"

M.C. yawned nonchalantly and butted her leg with his head a few times. "Mrow," was all he said.

"Look!" red-headed Andrew was insisting.

"Isn't it beautiful?" Michael added.

Crouching behind a lilac bush was another cat. It was the color of a Siamese—cream with dark brown legs, face, and tail. It had big blue eyes. But instead of short Siamese fur, its coat was very long. Michael was right—it was beautiful.

"What kind of cat is it?" Andrew asked.

"I don't know," Kelly Ann said. "I'm going inside to call Hillary. The two of you keep an eye on M.C. and the new cat. I'll bring some food out for both of them in just a minute."

She ran into the kitchen and dialed Hillary's number. Hillary answered right away.

"Hi," Kelly Ann said breathlessly, "it's me."

"M.C.?" Hillary said.

"He's back!" Kelly Ann told her.

"I knew he would be," Hillary said. She sounded very relieved. "Good old M.C."

"That's not all," Kelly Ann went on. "He's got another cat with him. I've never seen one like it. It must be a special breed."

"I'll be right over," said Hillary. "We can look it up in *Fabulous Felines*. Bye."

Fabulous Felines was a book Hillary's grand-

5

mother had sent her while she was at camp. "Because M.C. is the most fabulous feline I know," her grandmother had written.

Just now, M.C. was meowing demandingly through the McCoys' screen door. "You know you're not allowed inside," Kelly Ann answered. "I'm coming as fast as I can." She opened a bag of moist cat food, filled two dishes, and carried them outside. The new cat was still huddled behind the lilac bush.

"It's afraid," Michael said.

"How long is it going to stay in there?" Andrew asked.

"Maybe it'll come out to eat," Kelly Ann told them. She set down one of the dishes for M.C., who didn't wait for his guest to be served. He dug right in.

Kelly Ann knelt down and held the second dish out toward the new cat. It studied her face with its bright blue eyes for several seconds. Finally it must have decided that everything was okay, because it crept slowly out from behind the lilac.

"It's big!" Andrew said.

"It's furry as a bear," Michael added.

"Let's call it Bear," said Andrew.

Then the twins shouted: "Hey, Hillary!"

She was zooming up the driveway on her bike, her brown bangs standing straight up.

"Come see our new cat!"

"Ten minutes, forty-eight seconds," Hillary said, checking her watch. "I think I'll try out for the Olympics!" She leaned her bike against the fence and unstrapped the cat book from her carrying rack. "Hi, guys," she greeted the twins.

Hillary squatted down and took a good look at Bear, now eating almost as hungrily as M.C. "Definitely a Himalayan," said Hillary.

"A what?" Kelly Ann asked. She was trying to comb the tangles out of the cat's long hair with her fingers.

"A Himalayan," Hillary repeated. "I'll show you a picture in *Fabulous Felines.*" She opened the book and flipped past pages of bobtailed Manxes, lean Abyssinians, and wavy-haired Rexes. "There," she said. "It's part Persian and part Siamese—very fancy."

Kelly Ann looked at the glossy photograph of a long-haired cat lying on a dark-blue velvet pillow. "Too fancy to be tied up with a dirty old rope," she remarked. "Look at this."

Buried in the thick fur around Bear's neck was a piece of knotted cord. One end of it was ragged: "Like it's been chewed...." Kelly Ann said thoughtfully. Her eyes met Hillary's.

"Has M.C. brought us another mystery?" asked Hillary. She turned to M.C.: "Come on, Mystery Cat, stop stuffing your face and tell us about it."

She picked the gray cat up and pressed her

nose against his: "Where were you on the night of August fifteenth?" she said in a stern voice.

M.C. wriggled disgustedly, and the twins giggled. Then Hillary sniffed. "Hey!" she said.

"What?" said Kelly Ann. She was picking at the knots in the cord around Bear's neck.

"If this is a mystery—and it must be, or why else would M.C. be in on it?—anyway, if this is a mystery," Hillary continued, "I think M.C. has given us our first big clue." She handed a squirming M.C. to Kelly Ann. "Smell his fur," she instructed. "What does it smell like to you?"

Kelly Ann breathed in. A surprised look came into her eyes. She put M.C. down and sniffed at Bear.

"Well?" said Hillary.

At the same time, both girls said, "*Chocolate!*"

Chapter Two

"Do we get to keep him?" Andrew was asking about the Himalayan.

Hillary shook her head. "I'm afraid not, guys," she said.

"But we kept M.C.," Michael pointed out.

"This cat is not a stray," Kelly Ann explained to her brothers. "We have to find out who he belongs to." She pulled the frayed cord off the Himalayan's neck. "I think we'd better close him up in the garage," she told Hillary. "We don't want him to disappear before we can return him."

"Let's put M.C. in with him," Hillary suggested, "to keep him company."

Kelly Ann carried the Himalayan, and Hillary carried a protesting M.C. into the small garage. Then the girls went into the house to look at the lost-and-found column of the last few issues of the *Windsor Watchman*. Someone had lost a briefcase, and someone else had found a kitten. But there was no mention of a purebred Himalayan, lost *or* found.

"Let's try Mrs. Green at the animal shelter," Hillary said. She picked up the phone in the Mc-

Coys' kitchen and dialed. "Hello, this is Hillary Barnett. . . .Yes, Mrs. Green, he came back this afternoon. Has anyone reported a missing Himalayan? Because M.C. brought one home with him. . . .Okay. . . ." Hillary turned to Kelly Ann. "She's checking her list. . . .Yes? Mrs. Richard Gill," Hillary repeated as she wrote, "49 Pin Oak Road . . .495-8203. Thanks . We'll try her."

Hillary hung up the phone. "Three days ago, this Mrs. Gill reported her Himalayan missing. But then she called the shelter back to say he'd turned up."

"Maybe we should phone her anyway," Kelly Ann proposed. "There can't be that many Himalayans in Windsor. She may be able to give us the names of other owners."

"That's what Mrs. Green said." Hillary handed the phone to Kelly Ann. "Your turn."

Kelly Ann dialed Mrs. Gill's number and held the phone so Hillary could hear, too. It rang three times. Finally a woman answered.

"Hello, my name is Kelly Ann McCoy," Kelly Ann said. "May I speak to Mrs. Gill?"

"This is she," the woman replied.

"I understand you lost a Himalayan—" Kelly Ann began.

"Please bring him at once," the woman interrupted her brusquely. "I've done as you told me with the money."

Money? Kelly Ann and Hillary looked at

11

each other. But Mrs. Gill had hung up the phone.

"What do you suppose she meant by that?" Hillary asked.

"I thought she'd already found her cat," said Kelly Ann, puzzled, as she placed the receiver back in its cradle.

"Maybe she has more than one Himalayan," Hillary said. "Do you know where Pin Oak Road is?" The Barnetts had lived in Windsor for less than a year. Hillary didn't know her way around quite as well as Kelly Ann did.

Kelly Ann nodded. "Dad added a sunporch to a house on Pin Oak last summer," she said, "and I went with him once."

"Great," said Hillary. "Let's put the cat in a cardboard box and ride over there."

"We have to wait for Mom to come back," Kelly Ann told her. Mrs. McCoy was dropping off some papers at the insurance company where she worked part-time, so Kelly Ann had to keep an eye on Andrew and Michael.

The girls didn't have to wait long. Mrs. McCoy's old car soon chugged up the driveway. Then they heard the twins' excited voices, telling their mother all about Bear.

Mrs. McCoy opened the back door and smiled at the girls. She was a thin woman, with blond hair like Kelly Ann's and a pleasant face. "Hello, Hillary," she said. "The boys tell me that

M.C. has brought home a friend?" She looked inquisitively at Kelly Ann.

"Don't worry, Mom," her daughter reassured her. "I haven't adopted another cat. We think we've found his owner already—we're taking him over there now on our bikes."

As soon as the garage door was opened M.C. shot through it and ran up a tree.

"He didn't like having the door shut," Michael observed solemnly.

"He must remember when Mom and I bathed him," Kelly Ann told Hillary with a grin. "It was the only time we've closed the garage door on him."

But the Himalayan was curled up on a stack of old newspapers, his eyes half shut. "He's worn out, poor thing," Kelly Ann said. "Who knows what he's been through?"

The cat didn't complain at all when the girls lifted him into a cardboard box and tied it closed. They fastened the box to the back of Kelly Ann's bike with more twine.

"Back soon," Kelly Ann called to her mother. They were off to Mrs. Gill's house.

Pin Oak Road curved away from Main Street, following the shoreline of Mill Pond. Forty-nine Pin Oak was an old brick house with green shutters and a flagstone walk.

The girls leaned their bikes against a big tree in front. Hillary held Bear's box while Kelly Ann

13

pressed the doorbell.

The chimes had hardly stopped ringing when the door flew open. A plump, gray-haired woman stood there, glaring down at them. "How *old* are you?" she asked sharply.

The girls looked at each other, surprised. "Eleven," they said.

"Is that my cat?" the woman demanded, staring at the box Hillary was carrying. At the sound of her voice, Bear started to mew excitedly.

Before either girl could answer her, the woman jerked the box out of Hillary's hands. "Come with me," the woman said. She led them into an overfurnished living room. "Wait here," she ordered. Then she left with the box and the cat, pushing the door closed behind her.

"You'd think she'd be a little nicer," Hillary said indignantly. "I mean, after all, we *did* bring her cat back."

Kelly Ann nodded. She wandered over to the window and peered out. "Hey, there's a police car in front!"

Hillary joined her at the window. "What's going on?" she said.

With that, the living room door flew open. "Here they are, officer," the plump woman was saying. "Not ten minutes after I delivered the ransom money, I got a phone call from these two. Then they waltzed right in with my cat!"

Chapter Three

"Ransom money?" Hillary repeated, astonished.

Kelly Ann just stared, dumbfounded.

"I suppose you don't know anything about this note, either!" the woman said angrily. She waved a folded piece of paper. "Although what two girls your age need with that much money is beyond me!"

"What is she talking about?" Hillary demanded. Both girls looked to the young policeman for an explanation.

"You'd all better come with me to the station," he said. "I'm sure we'll be able to clear this up." But he looked a little doubtful.

He loaded the girls' bikes into the trunk of the police car. Then the plump lady got into the front seat. Hillary and Kelly Ann sat in the back, behind a wire grid that made them feel as though they were already in jail.

"I think M.C. has done it again," Hillary murmured to Kelly Ann.

Kelly Ann agreed. She whispered back: "I know what you mean. But I don't know if this is a mystery or just a *mess*."

"Do you think it's time to call our lawyer?" Hillary asked her, giggling. She meant her father, Mr. Barnett.

The girls were in luck. Behind the desk at the Windsor Police Station was their old friend Sergeant Thomas. "Misses McCoy and Barnett!" he greeted them with a big smile. "What brings you here? That cat of yours up to something again?"

The plump lady looked down her nose at them. "They're here," she said frostily, "for kidnapping my Tupten Kanchenjunga. And extorting five hundred dollars from me!"

Sergeant Thomas looked at her blankly. "Tupten Kanchen—?" He turned to the young policeman. "Willis?" he said inquiringly.

Officer Willis answered, "This is Mrs. Richard Gill, Sergeant. She claims these girls stole her cat and then took five hundred dollars to return it."

Kelly Ann's face had flushed a bright red with embarrassment. Hillary's face was red, too —but she was angry! She started to blurt something out.

The sergeant held up his hand. "Mrs. Gill," he told the woman, "I know these girls. They helped me recently on a counterfeiting case. I think you've made some kind of mistake. But let's hear your side of things first."

17

"Every evening, I let Tupten, my Himalayan, out of the house for his evening constitutional," Mrs. Gill began. "He usually stays outside for ten minutes or so, then meows to be let back in. Three evenings ago, he never came back. I called and called. I searched the whole neighborhood in my car. But he had disappeared, as if the earth had swallowed him up!" she said grimly.

"Early the next morning, I phoned the animal shelter to report him missing. That was before I found *this* in my mailbox!" She took a piece of yellow paper out of her handbag and passed it to Sergeant Thomas.

He looked at it quickly, then held it out to Hillary and Kelly Ann. "Have you girls seen this before?" he asked.

The message was pieced together from letters cut out of a newspaper. IF YOU WANT TO SEE YOUR CAT ALIVE, it said, TELL NO ONE ABOUT THIS. GET TOGETHER FIVE HUNDRED DOLLARS IN OLD BILLS.

"Old bills are much harder to trace," Hillary muttered. In the past she hadn't been much of a reader. But since Mystery Cat had come into her life, Hillary had read every mystery book and crime story she could get her hands on. "With M.C. around, it pays to be informed," she had said to Kelly Ann.

The message ended with: YOU WILL BE TOLD WHERE TO DROP OFF THE MONEY.

The girls gave the yellow paper back to the

sergeant and shook their heads. Of course they had never seen it before.

Mrs. Gill went on, "I called the animal shelter back immediately and told them I'd found Tupten. Then I waited. I've been a nervous wreck!"

Kelly Ann looked at the woman a little more sympathetically. She knew how awful *she* had felt when M.C. disappeared for a day or two. And he had never been cat-napped!

"Finally," Mrs. Gill said, "this morning, I found another note pushed under my door." She handed the sergeant the folded paper she had waved at Hillary and Kelly Ann.

He read it and showed it to the girls. PUT THE FIVE HUNDRED DOLLARS IN A HANDBAG, the note said. AT 2 O'CLOCK, CROSS THE ROAD. MAKE SURE YOU ARE NOT FOLLOWED. WALK WEST AROUND MILL POND. THROW THE BAG INTO THE BUSHES BEHIND THE BOATHOUSE.

"You followed the instructions, Mrs. Gill?" Sergeant Thomas asked.

"Certainly," Mrs. Gill replied, "to the letter. I wouldn't do anything to endanger the life of my Tupten!"

"Did you see anyone near the pond?" he asked.

"Not really. A few children feeding the ducks and a man selling ice cream. Nothing out of the ordinary."

Sergeant Thomas turned to the young officer who had brought them all to the station. "Willis, take Hughes with you. Search the brush behind the boathouse for a handbag. What color is it, Mrs. Gill?"

"Black," she answered.

"Look for a black handbag, footprints, or anything else that might be helpful," the sergeant said. Willis and Hughes were out the door of the station in a hurry. "Go on," Sergeant Thomas said to Mrs. Gill.

"I wasn't back in the house ten minutes after leaving the ransom money when my telephone rang," Mrs. Gill said accusingly. "It was a girl named Kelly Ann McCoy, saying she had my cat."

"*No*," Hillary interrupted, "saying we knew you had lost a Himalayan."

"M.C. brought a cat home this afternoon," Kelly Ann began to explain to Sergeant Thomas.

"Ah, M.C.!" the sergeant said. "I knew he'd pop up in this somewhere."

Kelly Ann nodded. "He'd been gone for a few days, too. When he turned up at my house this afternoon, he had a cat with him. It looked like a Siamese with long hair. And it had a torn peice of rope knotted around its neck."

"Hmmm," said Sergeant Thomas. "Tied up, maybe, and somehow escaped."

"I checked the cat out in a book I have," Hillary continued the story. "It was definitely a Himalayan, which is a pretty valuable cat. So we called the animal shelter to see if anyone had reported one missing recently."

"Mrs. Green told us that a Mrs. Gill had phoned in about a Himalayan being lost, and then about it being found," Kelly Ann said.

"And since there can't be that many Himalayans in Windsor, we decided to call her anyway," Hillary said. "We thought she might be able to give us the names of other Himalayan owners."

"Instead, she told us to bring the cat over to her house," Kelly Ann said.

"Then she practically had us arrested," Hillary added. "I know we get one phone call — may I call my father now?"

"I don't think you'll need a lawyer, Hillary," Sergeant Thomas said with a smile. He turned to Mrs. Gill. "I can assure you that these girls had nothing to do with the kidnapping," he told her. "In fact, you're very lucky your cat ended up at the McCoys' house. It's unlikely that it would have been returned to you, even though you paid the ransom. The kidnapper probably would have dumped it out somewhere—or worse.

"Now, I'll have one of our officers run you home," he said to the woman. "If I find out anything at all about who stole your cat, I promise that I'll let you know."

"Thank you," Mrs. Gill said. She faced the girls. "I'm very pleased to have gotten my cat back," she said stiffly. But they could tell she still had her suspicions about them.

"Do you two need a ride home?" Sergeant Thomas asked Kelly Ann and Hillary after Mrs. Gill had left.

"No, thank you," Kelly answered. "We've got our bikes. I think I saw Officer Willis put them in the rack outside."

But as they turned to go, Officers Willis and Hughes came through the door. "We found the handbag, Sarge," Hughes said. "Behind the boathouse, right in the middle of the biggest patch of brambles. It was empty, of course."

"The kidnapper took the money out and threw away the bag," Willis added. The policeman had it dangling from the end of a stick.

"So he won't mess up the prints," Hillary explained to Kelly Ann in an undertone.

"Unfortunately," Sergeant Thomas said, taking a closer look at the handbag, "it's very rough leather. Prints won't show up well—if there are any. The kitty-napper might very likely have been wearing gloves."

"We'd better go," Kelly Ann said to Hillary. "Mom is going to be wondering where I am."

"And I promised George I'd play tennis with him as soon as he gets home from the office this

afternoon," Hillary said.

George was Hillary's father. She always referred to her parents by their first names, which had startled Kelly Ann the first few times she heard it. But she'd gotten used to it, although she couldn't imagine herself saying to her own parents, "Hi, Eileen, what's for lunch?" or, "What did you work on today, Kevin?" Just thinking of how her parents would react made Kelly Ann grin.

"Girls, you and M.C. have done your good deed for the week, returning Mrs. Gill's cat," the sergeant said. "I'm sure she's grateful—she was just a little upset. Anyway, thanks again for your help."

As they pulled their bikes out of the rack outside the police station, Kelly Ann said, "We found the Himalayan's owner, so M.C.'s latest mystery is solved."

"With a cat-napper still running around Windsor?" Hillary said. "We do have a great clue — the cats smelling like chocolate. Talk to you tomorrow," she called over her shoulder as she rode toward her house.

Kelly Ann pedaled thoughtfully home in the opposite direction.

Chapter Four

When Hillary called Kelly Ann early the next day, she asked, "Did M.C. come up with any more clues?"

"No," Kelly Ann answered. "Did he give you any?"

"Are you kidding?" Hillary said. "He's cat-napping himself, sprawled all over his pillow at the end of my bed. His feet are up in the air and he's snoring his head off. Mysteries are the farthest thing from his mind. Listen, I'm going shopping at the mall. I have to buy my grandmother a birthday present. Want to come?"

"I can't this morning," Kelly Ann said. "I told Mom I'd help her paint the new shelves in the twins' room."

"What about this afternoon?" Hillary suggested. "Ask if you can stay for dinner and spend the night, too. Glynis and George are practicing for a party next week, so the food ought to be pretty interesting."

Hillary's parents sometimes cooked elaborate meals together. They usually tried out new menus at least once on the family before serving them at a dinner party. It was at Hillary's house that Kelly Ann had first had caviar on toast (she didn't really like it—too fishy), cassoulet (a very tasty French stew with sausages), and flan (delicious caramel custard).

"Hang on," Kelly Ann told her friend. She put the phone down and went to talk to her mother. She was back in a minute. "It's okay," Kelly Ann said. "Mom's not working this afternoon. And the twins will feed M.C. this evening. I just have to get home early tomorrow."

"Meet me in front of Waldron's at one-thirty," Hillary told her. Waldron's was a big department store.

"See you then," Kelly Ann said.

North Star Mall was crowded with people. Serious shoppers worked their way from one store to the next, their arms draped with shiny paper shopping bags. Kids gathered inside and outside the record store, listening to the loud music. Strollers wandered aimlessly about, staring into shop windows.

"I thought I'd try Waldron's first," Hillary said as she and Kelly Ann entered the store. "Keep an eye out for anything with butterflies on it. My grandmother loves butterflies."

"What about a scarf?" Kelly Ann suggested, holding up a silk one sprinkled with butterflies and daisies.

"That would be great," Hillary said, "if only I hadn't given her a scarf for Christmas. What do you think of this?" she asked, pointing to a gold belt with a butterfly belt buckle.

Kelly Ann wrinkled her nose.

"Yeah, I guess it is pretty awful," Hillary agreed.

The girls looked at gloves, wallets, and eyeglass cases. Then they sampled some of the perfumes, spraying themselves with scent from one bottle, then another, and another.

"The kind on my left wrist isn't bad," Kelly Ann said. "But is it Chanel Number Nineteen? Or is that on my right arm?"

"We'd better stop or I'm going to get a headache," Hillary said, sneezing. "Besides, perfume isn't a very original birthday present. Maybe we should think about something else for a while. A great idea may just come to us."

"Mom gave me money to buy new sneakers," Kelly Ann told her.

"Let's do that now," Hillary said.

A store four doors down from Waldron's specialized in sneakers and running shoes. And what did the girls see in the window? A pair of white leather sneakers with a tiny blue butterfly near the heel.

"Perfect!" Hillary shrieked.

"For your grandmother?" Kelly said doubtfully.

"Grams will love them!" Hillary assured her.

Hillary rushed in and had the sneakers gift wrapped. She also bought a pair of sneakers for herself, gray with a navy *V* on the side. After a lot of deliberation, Kelly Ann chose some blue ones with a white swirl.

Next they stopped into Pet-o-rama. Hillary picked out a catnip mouse—"M.C. would practically kill for catnip," she said—and Kelly Ann a large package of dried liver treats.

Then Hillary said, "I'd like a treat myself. Isn't there a candy store down at the end of the mall?"

Coco's Chocolatier was a tiny shop advertising "chocolates hand-dipped on the premises." There were two customers ahead of Hillary and Kelly Ann. The girls were examining the candy in the glass cases, trying to decide what they wanted to order, when they heard a strange noise.

"What was that?" Hillary said in a low voice.

"I'm not sure. . . . Listen, there it is again," Kelly Ann answered.

"It's a cat," said Hillary. "Can you tell where it's coming from?"

There was a door at the back of the candy store. The sign taped to it said DO NOT ENTER. Kelly Ann jerked her head in that direction. "It sounds as if it's coming from back there," she murmured.

"There's a dog, too!" Hillary exclaimed. "Hear it whining?"

Then there was a sort of strangled yowl. "And a different cat!" Kelly Ann said. "How could there be that much space back there?"

"Cages?" Hillary guessed.

The salesperson, a pretty young woman wearing a red-and-white-checked apron, was smiling and talking with the other customers.

"Why is she pretending she doesn't hear it?" Hillary asked suspiciously.

"It's probably nothing," Kelly Ann said. She scrutinized the salesperson. "She looks harmless."

"Yeah—so did Carol," Hillary muttered. Carol was the name of one of the counterfeiters who had taken Hillary prisoner. She moved closer to get a look at the young woman's name tag. Suddenly she drew in her breath with a gasp!

Hillary grabbed Kelly Ann's arm and dragged her out of the candy shop. "Her name is C ol, too!" she told Kelly Ann excitedly. "It has to ve fate—we've found the animal-napper!"

"Wel-l-l," Kelly Ann said somewhat doubtfully.

"Didn't we hear a cat yowling in there?" Hillary asked. "And a dog? And another cat?"

"Ye-e-es." Kelly Ann had to admit it was true.

"And what does this place smell like?" Hillary asked.

"Chocolate," Kelly Ann said. It was the only answer possible. And *chocolate* was the clue M.C. had given them. "But—"

Hillary cut her off. "We've got to get a look at that back room," she said. "It must be *full* of kidnapped pets!"

Chapter Five

"Don't you think it would be a lot more likely for a cat-napper to hide kidnapped pets out in the country or somewhere?" Kelly Ann said to Hillary. "Someplace where no one would hear them. Why keep them in the middle of a shopping mall?"

"For exactly that reason," Hillary told her. "No one would ever think to look here!"

"I don't know. . . ." Kelly Ann said, still not convinced. Unlike Hillary, she didn't like to rush into things.

"Did we hear two cats and a dog, or not?" Hillary asked her impatiently. "It's pretty unusual to have two cats and a dog closed up in the back room of a tiny candy store, isn't it?"

"Why don't we call Sergeant Thomas and ask him to look into it?" Kelly Ann asked.

"We don't have enough to go on yet," Hillary said. "You keep Carol distracted. I'm going to try to get into the back room from outside."

"No," Kelly Ann said firmly. "You took all the risks the last time M.C. got us into something. You distract Carol—I'll try to get in."

She wouldn't listen to any arguments from Hillary, either. "Hang on to my new sneakers, okay? And my pajamas," she told her friend, handing Hillary her shoulder bag. Then Kelly Ann headed for the door at the end of the mall.

Hillary peered through the window of the candy shop. The salesperson was finishing up with the second customer, taking his money and counting out his change. "I'd better get back in there," Hillary muttered, "and keep her busy."

"May I help you?" the red-and-white-checked Carol asked with a smile.

"Yes," Hillary replied. "I want to buy some candy. . .lots of candy." She stared into the nearest glass case. "Let's see—I'll take a quarter-pound of those strawberry creams. . .no, change that to coconut creams. . .and also a half pound of milk-chocolate-covered caramels. . .and a quarter pound of malted milk balls. . .and. . ."

Outside, Kelly Ann had walked down the far edge of the mall and ducked around in back of the line of stores. Her heart was already banging against her ribs.

Some of the stores had large metal garbage bins in back, others small private parking areas for their employees' cars.

"Just my luck!" Kelly Ann said to herself. Surrounding the back door of the candy store, there was a paved rectangle large enough for a small bin and a blue compact car. And the whole thing was nearly enclosed by an eight-foot-high hurricane fence with a padlocked gate!

Kelly Ann looked around nervously. There was no one in sight—but could she really climb the fence? Then a piteous howl from inside the store decided for her. She was going to find out what was going on in there!

Kelly Ann grabbed the wire mesh with both hands as high up as she could and stuck the toe of one sneaker into the fence. A car was coming! She let go of the wire and knelt down, untying and retying her shoelace.

The car passed by without slowing down. Kelly Ann stood up and clutched the wire fence again. She stuck her other toe into the mesh and pulled herself up. Now she could hold on to the pipe at the top.

Her left toe hooked firmly in the fence, she swung her right leg over the pipe. Then she stuck her right toe into the mesh. She swung her left leg over. Dropping to the pavement inside the enclosure, she tried to land quietly.

Kelly Ann's breath was coming in short gasps. She scrambled out of sight behind the blue car and tried to calm down.

"What would Sergeant Thomas say if he saw me now?" she wondered. Not to mention her parents. What Kelly Ann was doing was called "breaking and entering." In addition to her favorite stories about chivalry and knighthood, and books about animals, Kelly Ann had read a few mysteries herself.

The cat yowled again, and the dog whined. "Hang on, guys," Kelly Ann reassured them silently. "We'll get you out of here."

But what was that? It sounded like nothing so much as the squealing of a pig! A pig? "It must be like Noah's ark in there!" Kelly Ann thought.

Now more curious than scared, she crept around the car. The small barred window was too dirty to see through. Kelly Ann edged toward the narrow door behind the garbage bin.

Still crouching, she reached over her head for the doorknob. Slo-o-owly she turned it. The door wasn't locked! Carefully she pushed it a little...and stuck her head in through the opening.

The tiny room was empty! There were a few small boxes stacked against a wall and some large bags of sugar in one corner. But where were the cats, the dog, the pig?

"Hands up!" a voice shrieked. "I've got you covered!"

Terrified, Kelly Ann raised trembling arms over her head. *"This is it!'* she thought.

Then there was a painfully shrill whistle, followed by a yowl, a bark, and a grunt. Kelly Ann cautiously raised her eyes. A bird! It was a large black bird in a cage that hung from the ceiling

above Kelly Ann's head.

The bird cocked a beady yellow eye at Kelly Ann's pale face and whistled again. "Oh, boy!" it shrieked loudly, and ruffled its feathers.

"I've got to get out of here!" Kelly Ann's brain said. She could hear a voice from inside the store itself. Someone was coming! The voice prodded her along. In seconds she had scaled the wire mesh fence and dropped down safely on the other side of it.

There was just one problem. The sneaker she had untied and retied was stuck in the wire on the *inside* of the fence.

No time to try to retrieve it. Wearing the remaining sneaker, Kelly Ann sprinted around the corner of the mall and collapsed on a bench set in some shrubbery. Her heart was pounding in her ears.

"Kelly Ann—are you okay?" It was an anxious Hillary, loaded with shopping bags. "And what happened to your shoe?"

"I don't want to talk about it," Kelly Ann said. "Some kidnapper! All that noise? It was one bird!"

"Yeah, I know," Hillary said sympathetically. "It's Paco, Caron's mynah. She's going on vacation tomorrow, and she's boarding her bird at the pet store."

"Caron, huh?" Kelly Ann said.

"When I got close to her, I saw that her name

wasn't Carol," Hillary admitted. "It was Caron."

"For that I lost a shoe"—how was she going to explain that to her mother?—"and practically had a heart attack!" Kelly Ann grumbled.

"Luckily, you have a new pair of sneakers right here," Hillary pointed out brightly. She put the shopping bag down at Kelly Ann's feet. Then she dropped ten little red bags tied with ribbon onto the bench.

"What's all that?" Kelly Ann asked.

"Candy," Hillary said. "Twelve dollars worth. It was the only way I could think of to keep Caron busy while you were looking around." She tore open a bag. "Eat the caramels first, okay? They get stuck in my braces."

"I never want to see, smell, or taste chocolate again," Kelly Ann said later, as they rode up the sidewalk to Hillary's house.

Hillary agreed. "I think I've gained ten pounds in the last hour," she moaned, climbing off her bike and falling flat on the lawn. "I feel like an overstuffed sofa."

"Hi, girls!" Mr. Barnett called through the front door. "You're just in time to take a look at tonight's pièce de la résistance: dessert."

"What is it?" Hillary asked from her prone position on the grass.

"One of your favorites," her father called back. *Chocolate mousse!*

Chapter Six

Somehow Kelly Ann and Hillary got through the dinner. First there were artichokes with lemon butter. Next came a clear soup. Then Glynis and George served a roast stuffed with veal kidneys, which sounded awful but tasted fairly good, and a green salad. Finally the girls struggled through dessert.

They complimented Hillary's parents on their menu. Then they walked, very slowly, down the hall to Hillary's room and eased themselves onto the bed.

"Thank goodness Mrs. Griffis stayed late to help clean up," Hillary groaned. Mrs. Griffis was the Barnetts' housekeeper. "Scraping plates and looking at food one second longer would have made me sick."

"I think it's going to take me three days just to digest all this," Kelly Ann said.

They listened to some records for a while. Then they looked at Hillary's yearbook.

Hillary and Kelly Ann were in the same grade. But Kelly Ann went to the Windsor Middle School and Hillary went to Lincoln Country

Day, a private school in a neighboring town.

"He's cute," Kelly Ann said, pointing to the picture of a dark-haired boy in Hillary's class.

"Incredibly conceited," Hillary told her. "But this one's okay, even if he is kind of goofy-looking. And she's nice."

"Hey, there's a picture of you with M.C.!" Kelly Ann said.

"Yeah, George took it right after M.C. came here," Hillary said. "Funny old cat. Did you ever see a nicer expression?" she added fondly. In the photograph Hillary was holding M.C. under his front legs. The cat was scowling at the camera, his left hind foot raised, trying to scratch Hillary's hand.

Kelly Ann yawned sleepily and looked at the clock on the bureau. "It's after eleven. Shouldn't M.C. be getting here soon from my house?"

Hillary shook her head. "No, it's usually closer to twelve or twelve-thirty," she answered. "Maybe we should wait up for him."

But they both fell asleep, on top of the covers, with all their clothes on.

Kelly Ann was dreaming about the wire-mesh fence. No matter how high she climbed, the pipe at the top was always the same distance away. She was never going to reach it!

Behind her someone was shouting, "Stop in the name of the law!" A black bird with yellow eyes was flapping around her head. And some-

where a cat was yowling angrily. . .and yowling
. . .and yowling. . .

Kelly Ann opened her eyes. For just a second, she didn't remember where she was. Then she saw Hillary asleep on the bed next to hers. Mrs. Barnett must have come in and turned out the lights, because the bedroom was dark and a quilt covered each girl.

A cat *was* yowling! Kelly Ann looked at the clock—12:35. Could it be M.C., in some kind of trouble?

"Hillary!" Kelly Ann said urgently. "Wake up!"

"Hmph?" Hillary grunted.

"Listen!" Kelly Ann urged.

The yowling rose and fell. Suddenly Hillary was wide awake. "M.C.!" she said.

Hillary threw back the quilt and sprang to the window. She pushed it wide open and stuck her head out.

"Where is he?" she asked. There was nothing in the circle of light cast by the street lamp. Hillary leaned as far out of the window as she could, trying to see down the street. Her hand slipped and with a shriek, Hillary somersaulted out the window!

"Ooooph!" She hit the ground with a muffled thud.

"Are you all right?" Kelly Ann whispered anxiously. It was so dark that she couldn't see her friend very well among the mounded shapes of plants.

"Yes!" Hillary whispered back. "I fell into the azaleas. Come on—hurry!" She climbed to her feet and ran down the driveway.

"It's a good thing we're still dressed," Kelly Ann thought as she lowered herself, feet first, out the bedroom window. "And a good thing that Hillary lives in a one-story house." Kelly Ann set off down the Barnetts' driveway after her friend.

She could just make out Hillary's pale-yellow shirt as Hillary cut across a neighboring lawn. Kelly Ann followed, but after four strides she tripped over a sprinkler and pitched forward onto the grass.

Kelly Ann felt a sharp pain in her right ankle. When she stood up and put her weight on it, the pain increased. "Twisted it," she murmured.

Hillary had disappeared into the darkness. There was another angry yowl from M.C., farther down the street. Kelly Ann limped as fast as she could in that direction. If only there were a moon tonight, maybe she could see something!

Suddenly Kelly Ann spotted someone wearing white trousers near the end of the wide, dead-end street. A pair of ghostly legs crouched, moved backward, and then stepped forward in the darkness.

Hillary knew she didn't have much farther

to go when M.C. yowled again. She changed her direction a little, noticing a figure between herself and the carriage lamp at the end of the McConnells' yard. The person was silhouetted against the light. Hillary was pretty sure it was a man. And she could just make out a small shape more solid than the surrounding night: M.C.! Was the man dragging M.C. along at the end of a rope? She remembered the frayed cord around the Himalayan's neck.

"You stop that!" Hillary shouted into the darkness.

The figure froze. M.C. gave a loud hiss and a snarl and bounded up the street toward Hillary. He scooted past her and tore across the lawn toward the Barnetts' house.

Hillary, fearless with anger, ran down the street toward the man in white trousers. Suddenly a set of headlights flicked on. A motor roared to life, and with a screech of tires, a truck headed straight at her.

"If I stand here, he'll have to stop," Hillary thought. "And *this* mystery will be solved." But at almost the same instant, she thought, "Am I crazy?"

Hillary leaped for the safety of a nearby yard.

The truck zoomed past without slowing and sped up the street.

Chapter Seven

The truck's headlights swept across Kelly Ann's face, blinding her for an instant. Still she was able to make out the last two numbers on the rear license plate, sort of.

"They were either two three's, two eight's, eighty-three, or thirty-eight," she told Hillary, who helped her hobble up the street.

"That's better than nothing," Hillary said. "At least we have something to go on. And what about the truck? It was white, right?"

"Or cream. Or maybe light blue," Kelly Ann said. "It's hard to tell in the dark."

By the time the two girls had made it to the Barnetts' front walk, there was at least one light on in every house on the block.

"I guess we got a little noisy," Hillary commented.

Her house was completely lit up. Mrs. Barnett was standing on the front steps in a striped robe, peering into the darkness. "Hillary, is that you?" she called.

"Is she going to yell at us?" Kelly Ann wondered. She knew that *her* parents would be pretty annoyed if she decided to go for a stroll at one in the morning.

But when Hillary answered, "Yes, Glynis. Kelly Ann's twisted her ankle." Mrs. Barnett hurried down the walk toward them.

"First that terrible yowling, then shouting, then the shriek of tires! We couldn't imagine what was going on," Mrs. Barnett said, taking Kelly Ann's other arm. "George went to your room, Hillary, but you were gone. The window was wide open, and M.C. was on your bed, bleeding onto your pillow. . . ."

"M.C.'s bleeding!" Hillary exclaimed.

"Is he badly hurt?" Kelly Ann asked. She started to hop up the walk on her good leg.

"Not badly as Hillary's father is," Mrs. Barnett replied. "M.C. has a little cut on his ear. But he gave George a good scratch when he got too close to the bed."

As they reached the steps, the front door was flung open and Mr. Barnett came tearing out of the house. He had a powerful flashlight in one hand, a poker from the fireplace in the other. His shirttail was flapping outside his trousers.

"They're okay," his wife reassured him. "But Kelly Ann has twisted her ankle."

Mr. Barnett put the poker down and took a deep breath. He eyed the girls and said calmly, "Suppose you tell us exactly what is going on here."

"I'm not sure," Hillary admitted. "We heard M.C. yowling outside and went to see about him. I thought maybe someone was trying to kidnap him and hold him for ransom."

"Like the Himalayan you found?" her father asked.

Hillary and Kelly Ann nodded.

"I know M.C. is a very special cat," Mr. Barnett said to the two of them. "Very special," he repeated, rubbing two long scratches on his arm. "But he doesn't really look like a good prospect for ransom, does he?"

"Then why was that guy trying to drag him into the truck?" Hillary asked.

Mr. Barnett's expression was grim. "Are you telling me there was a man out there—" he began.

"Let's talk about this inside. I want to look at Kelly Ann's ankle," said Mrs. Barnett.

She sat Kelly Ann down on the couch and started to untie her tennis shoe.

"I'll do it," Kelly Ann told her. She winced as she pulled off her shoe and sock.

"Does it hurt?" Hillary asked.

"A little," Kelly Ann admitted.

"It's quite swollen," Mrs. Barnett said. There was a large, soft lump on the outside of Kelly Ann's right foot, just above the ankle joint. It was starting to turn blue. "We'd better put some ice on that," Mrs. Barnett decided.

"Would you mind if I saw M.C. first?" Kelly Ann asked.

"We'll all see M.C.," Mrs. Barnett answered. "Let's go to Hillary's room. Kelly Ann can lie down and put her foot up."

M.C. was enthroned on his pillow at the end of Hillary's bed. He yawned and stretched when he saw the girls. "Mew," he said delicately, as though he couldn't imagine what all the fuss was about. As Hillary took a look at his cut, he began to purr loudly.

"It *would* have to be his good ear," Kelly Ann muttered. She examined it closely. "It's okay," she told Hillary. "It's a small cut. And it's already stopped bleeding."

Mrs. Barnett made Kelly Ann comfortable on the other bed. She brought in some extra pillows to prop up Kelly Ann's leg, and a plastic bag filled with ice cubes for her ankle.

"All right, George," Mrs. Barnett said to her husband. "Let's take care of your scratches."

"No more adventures in the dead of night," Mr. Barnett said to the girls. "I don't know what the man in the truck had to do with M.C., or vice versa. But I want you both *out* of it." He faced his daughter. "Is that understood, Hillary? Tomorrow you will call Sergeant Thomas and tell him what happened here. And that is the end of your involvement in this mess. I mean it."

"Oh, George," Hillary grumbled.

47

"I'm serious," he said firmly. "Tomorrow you'll speak to the sergeant. Then you'll forget the whole thing. Good night."

As the girls put on their pajamas, Hillary said, "I don't know what's wrong with *him*. He doesn't usually carry on so much."

"He's probably remembering the last time, with the counterfeiters," Kelly Ann told her.

"Maybe," Hillary said. "Boy, am I tired!" She straightened the sheets on her bed and slid into it. "Yuck!" she exclaimed, hurriedly drawing her legs up. "M.C., what did you drop in my bed?"

Hillary felt around at the end of the mattress, and pulled out a small cloth bag with a long piece of string attached.

"What is that?" Kelly Ann asked.

"Look at the way M.C. is acting," Hillary said.

The big gray cat rubbed his face and head all over the bag. Then he reached out with his paw and tried to hook it away from Hillary.

"If it isn't catnip," Hillary said, "it's something just like it."

"But where did he get it?" Kelly Ann wondered.

"Maybe," Hillary said, "this is what he was fighting with the man about!"

"Maybe that *was* the cat-napper out there," said Kelly Ann excitedly. "Maybe he uses catnip to get cats into his truck."

Chapter Eight

The day before—after all the chocolate candy, plus the Barnetts' big dinner—Kelly Ann and Hillary had thought they wouldn't be able to eat again for at least a week. But now, at breakfast, they each managed to get down three of Mrs. Griffis's blueberry pancakes.

M.C. had already been served his morning meal in Hillary's bedroom—leftover roast beef stuffed with veal kidneys, and a side dish of cream. He had washed his face thoroughly and settled down to a long nap, his head resting on the mysterious bag of catnip.

Kelly Ann's ankle was a little less swollen this morning. "But you're not going to ride home like that," Mrs. Barnett decided. "I'll drop you and your bike off at your house on the way to the Landmarks Preservation Society." Although she lived in a very modern house herself, Mrs. Barnett was interested in preserving the old buildings in Windsor.

"And Hillary," Mrs. Barnett added as she and Kelly Ann prepared to leave, "please call Sergeant Thomas as your father asked you to."

Hillary decided to ride her bike over to the police station, instead of calling. After a tussle with M.C., who very definitely didn't want to give it up, she took the cloth bag along as evidence.

Sergeant Thomas was in, and he listened attentively to Hillary's story. But when she had finished he said, "We don't have much to go on. The last two numbers of the license plate were either thirty-three, eighty-eight, eighty-three, or thirty-eight. The color of the truck was either pale blue, cream, or white. Was it a pickup truck?" he asked.

"I'm not sure," Hillary said. She had been too busy scrambling out of the way to get a good look at it. "I think it might have been a panel truck."

"And this," Sergeant Thomas said, looking at the cloth bag M.C. had brought home, "seems to be made of an old cotton handkerchief. There are no marks on it of any kind. I'll have it tested, but I'm fairly certain that the stuff inside is catnip."

Hillary agreed. M.C. had pretty well proved that.

"Are there any valuable cats down at the end of your street?" the sergeant asked.

Hillary hadn't thought of that. She had been too concerned about M.C. to consider that someone else's cat might have been the real target.

"Let's see," she said. "The McConnells have a poodle, no cats. But the Garsons have a Siamese. . . .That's it! The Garsons' lilac-point Siamese! I saw it this morning, asleep on the front porch. M.C. must have kept the cat-napper from grabbing it!"

"Mmmm—could be," the sergeant said. "Well, we'll put an extra patrol car in your area, and we'll be on the lookout for any light-colored truck that seems to be parked where it shouldn't be. Please call us if you — or M.C. — notice anything out of the ordinary."

Hillary left the police station and rode over to the McCoys'. But before she had even climbed off her bike, the twins dashed outside.

"Hillary! Kelly Ann has been phoning and phoning you!" Andrew shouted. Samantha was running in circles around him, barking loudly.

"M.C.'s been hurt!" Michael added.

"What!" Hillary couldn't believe what she was hearing. She had just left him, not much more than an hour ago, safely asleep on her bed.

Kelly Ann hobbled out of the house. "He was hit by a car," she said, her voice shaking.

"How do you know?" Hillary asked her.

"He must have been on his way over here from your house," Kelly Ann told her. "Someone picked him up out of the street and carried him to Dr. Lufrano's office." Dr. Lufrano had been the McCoys' veterinarian for years. "She recognized him, and she called us."

"We'd better get over there right now!" Hillary exclaimed.

"Mom's not home," Kelly Ann said. "I've got to keep an eye on the twins. I don't think I can ride my bike very well, anyway, with this." She pointed to her ankle, now wrapped with an Ace bandage. "You go, and call me as soon as you've seen him!"

"Isn't Billy's mother home?" Hillary asked. Billy Johnson lived in the house next door and was the twins' best friend.

"Guys," Hillary suggested to Andrew and Michael, "why don't you ask Mrs. Johnson if you can stay with Billy for a little while—just until Kelly Ann and I can find out about M.C."

"Sure," the twins agreed, glancing sympathetically at their sister. They scooted down the steps, Samantha behind them.

It wasn't long before Mrs. Johnson called over the fence. "I'll be glad to watch the boys, Kelly Ann. Go on and see about your cat."

"You can sit on the crossbar of my bike," Hillary said to her friend. "I'll pedal you."

They talked very little on their way to the vet's. But Hillary did say, "Do you think it could have been—"

"I'm sure it wasn't," Kelly Ann answered quickly. "It was probably just a bad driver."

Dr. Lufrano hastily reassured the girls when

she saw their frightened faces. "M.C.'s going to be all right," she told them. "He's bruised and shaken up. But he's a tough old bird. There are no broken bones or fractures."

"Can we see him?" Hillary asked.

"Yes, for a minute," the veterinarian said. "He's a little groggy. I had to give him an anesthetic to examine him properly—he was fighting all the way."

"Good old M.C.," Hillary said fondly.

M.C. was lying on his side in a small cage in back. His eyes were closed, but he opened them a little when Kelly Ann spoke to him.

He meowed softly, acknowledging the girls' presence. Then he closed his eyes again.

"I want to keep him overnight," Dr. Lufrano said. "Just as a precaution. But if all goes well, and it should, you can take him home in the morning."

As she led them back to the reception area, Dr. Lufrano said, "M.C. was very lucky. He must have been jumping out of the way when the car struck him. It was a glancing blow, not a solid impact."

"Do you know who brought him in?" Kelly Ann asked.

"Yes," Dr. Lufrano said. "Mr. Rudin. He owns a dry cleaners on Elm Street. It happened right in front of his store."

"We ought to go thank him," Kelly Ann said

to Hillary on their way out the door.

"Definitely," Hillary agreed. "Dr. Lufrano," she added in a low voice to the veterinarian, "please send the bill to my parents—the McCoys paid last time." Last time was when M.C. had tangled with the counterfeiters.

Mr. Rudin was a short, cheerful man with a bristly beard. "Glad to do it," he said when the girls had told him how much they appreciated his taking M.C. to the doctor. "Actually, I thought he was a stray at first, with his torn ear and broken tail and all. But Dr. Lufrano told me he wasn't.

"The cat just lay there, stunned for a minute, the wind knocked out of him. I wrapped him in a towel and put him on the front seat of my car. Halfway to Dr. Lufrano's—she takes care of our Labrador—he started fighting the towel. He is some fighter!" Mr. Rudin grinned.

"Did you happen to see who hit him?" Hillary asked.

"As a matter of fact," Mr. Rudin answered. "I was standing in the doorway here, talking to a customer. So I was facing the street. The truck almost seemed to be *trying* to hit the cat—both wheels on the right side came way up on the sidewalk."

"Truck?" Hillary repeated. She suddenly got goosebumps.

"That's right, a truck," Mr. Rudin said deliberately. "A white panel truck."

Hillary and Kelly Ann exchanged glances. "You didn't see the license plate, did you?" Kelly Ann asked.

Mr. Rudin shook his head. "I was so surprised by what had happened that I didn't even think to look. The truck sped away. And I was mostly worried about the cat."

"What a nice man," Kelly Ann said as Hillary pedaled her back home.

"I'm going to tell Glynis to bring all our dry cleaning here, even if it is a little out of the way," Hillary said.

"Hillary," Kelly Ann said gravely, "I want to find the man who hit M.C."

"I have a feeling we will," Hillary answered.

Chapter Nine

But the girls would have to rely on someone other than Mystery Cat for their next clue. When Mrs. Barnett drove Hillary and Kelly Ann to pick the gray cat up the next morning, Dr. Lufrano suggested that he be kept inside for a few more days.

"M.C.'s not going to be happy about it," she told them. "He's used to making his daily rounds, going where he pleases. But as bruised as he is, he might not be able to jump out of harm's way if he had to," she explained to the girls.

"He can stay in my bedroom, okay?" Hillary said to Kelly Ann.

Kelly Ann agreed. At the McCoys', animals didn't sleep in the house. Samantha had her doghouse. And M.C. slept in a box in the garage —with the door open, of course. Even if a special exception were made this time, there were the twins to consider. With Andrew and Michael running in and out, M.C. might manage to escape from Kelly Ann's bedroom.

So M.C. rode home to the Barnetts'. Hillary

carried him back to her bedroom and settled him down on his pillow. She also latched the window so M.C. couldn't push it open.

"I'm kind of glad Dr. Lufrano suggested this," Kelly Ann told her. "At least we won't have to worry about the man in the truck finding M.C. again."

"Not if we find the guy first, before M.C. has recovered," Hillary added.

"Do you want to come to dinner tonight?" Kelly Ann asked her. "Daddy is making what he calls McCoyburgers and his special baked beans."

"You bet!" Hillary said. "Glynis and George and going to be practicing again for the party. I'd like some *real* food for a change!"

When Hillary's father dropped her off late that afternoon, Mr. McCoy and the kids were already gathered around the big stone barbecue he had built in the backyard. The twins came running when they saw her. Even lazy old Samantha opened one eye and woofed hello.

"It smells great," Hillary said as she walked across the yard to the grill.

"Hi, Hillary," Mr. McCoy said, deftly flipping a burger with a long-handled spatula. "I was just telling this mob that a great cook never reveals his recipes. If I told everyone about my top-secret ingredients, I would no longer be the best outdoor chef in the world." His crinkly mustache twitched as he grinned at her.

"Kevin," Mrs. McCoy called just then from inside the house, "is it time to add the Worcestershire sauce to the beans yet?"

"You didn't hear that," Mr. McCoy said, laughing. He trotted to the house to tend to the beans.

"How is M.C.?" Michael asked Hillary.

"Mean as a snake because I won't let him out of the bedroom," Hillary answered. "But otherwise he seems okay."

"Are you going to catch the guy who hit him?" Andrew asked.

"I hope so," Hillary replied. "But we need some more clues."

"No mysteries until after dinner," Mrs. McCoy said, putting down the big bowl of salad on the picnic table. "Hello, Hillary—maybe you could help me with the drinks, and Kelly Ann can sit down and rest her ankle."

"Oh, Mom, it's all right," Kelly Ann said.

"Sit down," her mother insisted. "Andrew, you and Michael bring out the knives and forks and the dinner plates. We're almost ready to eat."

Dinner at the McCoys' was informal and noisy, with the twins and Mr. McCoy swapping silly jokes, and Samantha pressing her cold nose onto Hillary's hand in hopes of a handout.

"It's nice having a big family," Hillary

remarked, looking around the table.

"This isn't big," Andrew spoke up. "In Daddy's family there were four boys and three girls. Or was it the other way around?"

"Listen!" Michael said. A tinkly melody was slowly growing louder. "Ice cream!"

"We have watermelon for dessert," Mr. McCoy reminded him. "Fresh from the garden."

"Ice cream," Andrew repeated firmly. "Please?"

"All right. Finish your salad first," Mrs. McCoy instructed.

Andrew stuffed a huge piece of tomato into his mouth. And Michael packed a handful of lettuce into his.

"We're done," Andrew tried to announce with his mouth crammed full.

"Not until you've swallowed all that," said their mother.

"Gross!" Kelly Ann said. "Still like the idea of a big family, Hillary?"

Mr. McCoy handed each of the boys two quarters.

"What kind are you getting?" Michael asked his twin as he clutched his money.

"Chocolate!" Andew answered.

"Me, too!" said Michael.

They rushed to the front yard to wait for the ice-cream truck.

Kelly Ann turned and looked at Hillary.

"What kind of truck is white...and smells like chocolate?" she asked suddenly.

"An ice-cream truck!" Hillary shrieked.

"May we be excused?" they both asked at once. Hillary jumped up from the table and raced out of the house. Kelly Ann limped after her.

The twins were standing in line with some other kids from the neighborhood at the white truck's side window. Large blue letters dripping with silver icicles announced "Ice Cream on Wheels." But it was the license number on the back of the truck that interested Hillary.

It was all wrong. "It's MSP six-four-seven-four," Hillary reported to Kelly Ann, who had just made it to the curb. "Not an eight or a three in the whole thing. And it was such a good idea!"

"But this can't be the only ice-cream truck in Windsor," Kelly Ann reasoned. "Let's see if there's a listing in the telephone book."

In the Yellow Pages under "Ice Cream and Frozen Desserts; Dealers," they found five names. Four were stores. But the fifth was "Travelin' Tom's Ice Cream on Wheels."

"Let's try it," Hillary said, picking up the phone. "Maybe he has more than one truck." She paused. "What am I going to say? I could actually be talking to the cat-napper!"

After thinking for a minute, she said, "Got

it." She dialed the number.

The phone was answered by Travelin' Tom himself.

"Could you tell me if you have a truck with a three and an eight in the license number?" Hillary asked.

"Why?" said Travelin' Tom.

"I put my books down for a minute on the back bumper of a white truck parked near Main Street," Hillary said hurriedly. "And it drove away with them. I was hoping it might be one of your ice-cream trucks."

"Nope. Not mine. In fact, not any ice-cream truck in Windsor," Travelin' Tom told her. "I'm the only ice cream on wheels in town."

"Are you sure it wasn't one of yours?" Hillary pressed him.

"Positive," Tom said. "I have six trucks. And their license numbers run in a series: six-four-seven-two, seven-three, seven-four, seven-five, seven-six, and seven-seven."

"Thanks," Hillary said. Discouraged, she hung up the phone. "Another dead end," she told Kelly Ann. "We're not getting anywhere with this."

"We do seem to do a lot better with M.C.'s help," Kelly Ann said gloomily.

Chapter Ten

The phone rang the next morning as Hillary was finishing her breakfast. She thought it might be Kelly Ann with some new ideas on the cat-napping case, so she raced to answer it.

But it wasn't Kelly Ann. "Hello, Hillary. Is your mother there?" Then the voice identified itself. "This is Mary Watson."

"Mrs. Watson," Hillary said, "I didn't recognize your voice. You sound different."

"Yes...well...I was supposed to go with your mother to a meeting of the Landmarks Commission. But I'm afraid I..."

"Wait just a minute," Hillary told her. "Here's Glynis."

"It's Mrs. Watson," she said to her mother, handing her the phone. Hillary walked back to the kitchen and her bowl of cereal and peaches.

"Mary?" said Mrs. Barnett. "...You aren't coming to the meeting?...Is anything wrong? You sound upset....No, only Hillary." Mrs. Barnett lowered her voice.

Hillary stopped chewing her Granola and listened.

"What?" Mrs. Barnett said. "Not Farrah Fawcett!"

Farrah Fawcett was one of Mary Watson's prize-winning Persians. If Hillary could have pricked up her ears, she would have.

Mrs. Barnett gasped. *"A ransom note?* Have you called the police?. . .I see. . . .Of course not . . . .What about her kittens?"

Farrah Fawcett had had a new litter of kittens earlier this summer.

". . .Bottle feeding," Mrs. Barnett said. ". . .No—I won't even tell George about it. You're sure you don't want to call the police?. . .Yes. . . . Please let me know if I can do anything. . . .Of course—I'll drive you as soon as you know where. But it may be several days—I've heard of such a case recently—tell you later. . . .Good-bye."

She walked into the kitchen, looking very preoccupied.

Hillary was ninety-nine percent certain that the cat-napper had struck again; that Mary Watson's Farrah had been cat-napped; and that Glynis had offered to drive her to drop off the ransom money!

But Hillary hoped that her mother might confirm her suspicions. "Mrs. Watson sounded weird," Hillary prompted.

"Mmmm," her mother answered guardedly. "I'm going to a meeting, Hillary," she said. "I should be back around eleven-thirty. I would like you to stay at home and go through your fall clothes for school. And be sure to let me know about any phone calls I may get."

Any other time, Hillary would have protested strongly about staying indoors on a beautiful day at the end of summer. Now she couldn't have been paid to leave.

And so began the famous Glynis-watch. Hillary stuck close to the house to keep an eye on her mother. When Glynis left to go shopping or to a meeting, Hillary guarded the phone.

"This is the plan," Hillary told Kelly Ann over the phone. "As soon as Mary Watson calls, Glynis will get into her car and go to pick her up. I'll jump on my bike and ride to Mrs. Watson's the back way, down the alley. I'll get there first, hide in the bushes, and try to eavesdrop."

"What if you don't hear where they're going before they drive away?" Kelly Ann asked.

"Then I'll just have to tail them on my bike," Hillary replied. "No problem. You know how fast I am."

"What am I supposed to be doing?" Kelly Ann asked.

"When they stop the car, I'll call you. If there isn't a phone booth around, I'll ask to use the phone in someone's house—tell them it's an emergency or something."

"Not too much of one, I hope," Kelly Ann murmured.

Hillary stayed at her house, and Kelly Ann at hers, waiting for a phone call. One day passed, then another. Glynis heard from Mrs. Watson a couple of times. But the calls seemed to be false alarms, because nothing happened.

Hillary was beginning to get as stir crazy as M.C. was. The tough old cat had taken to crouching at the edge of the door to Hillary's bedroom. When Hillary pushed the door open to walk into the room, M.C. would hurl himself through the opening and try to race down the hall to freedom.

The first time it happened, Hillary had to fling herself on him full-length, without stopping to consider his bruises. The second time she managed to grab his crooked tail on the way past. M.C. hissed and spat and growled as she hauled him backward into his prison. Hillary was beginning to feel pretty grumpy herself.

"How long are you going to keep this up?" Kelly Ann asked her on the morning of the third day.

"As long as it takes," Hillary said stubbornly.

"But this is the day M.C. goes back for his checkup," Kelly Ann reminded her. "Mom said she'd drive us."

"You'll have to go without me," Hillary said. "If the cat-napper behaves the way he did with

Mrs. Gill, today *has* to be the day for the ransom drop-off. This time we're going to get him, I just know it."

Kelly Ann and her mother arrived at the Barnetts' an hour later in Mrs. McCoy's old car. They loaded M.C. into the back seat, and Kelly Ann sat down next to him.

"Your bandage is off," Hillary noticed.

"The swelling is down," Kelly Ann said. "Are you sure you don't want to come?"

"I'd better not," Hillary answered discreetly. Mrs. McCoy got a little nervous about the girls' mysteries. "Call when you get home to tell me what Dr. Lufrano said."

The veterinarian pronounced M.C. perfectly fit and ready to rejoin the outside world. "I know there's no way to keep him from roaming," she told Kelly Ann, "so we'll just have to trust his instinct for self-preservation. He's done very well with it so far."

At the McCoys' house, M.C. reacquainted himself with some of his favorite spots, like the inside of Samantha's doghouse, after evicting the rightful owner. Everything was back to normal.

Kelly Ann called Hillary to report in. "Hear anything?" she asked then.

"No," Hillary replied glumly. "I've reread *Fabulous Felines* three times already. I'm getting pretty tired of fancy cats."

"What about going to the park with me?" Kelly Ann asked her. "Dad and the twins are playing in a neighborhood baseball game."

Hillary said no. "Glynis is supposed to be back in an hour. I have to be ready to tail her."

"Then I won't stay at the park long," Kelly Ann promised. "In forty-five minutes I'll be back at my house, waiting to hear from you."

But even the best plans don't always work out.

Chapter Eleven

"Are you ready, Kelly Ann?" the twins called when she hung up the phone.

"We're leaving, honey," her father said.

"Go ahead," Kelly Ann told them. "I'll catch up with you. I want to look for my camera."

"Good," Andrew said as he went out the door. "You can take a picture of me hitting a home run."

Kelly Ann dug through her desk drawers until she found it. "Only six exposures left," she murmured. "I'll use them up today."

Kelly Ann slipped the camera strap onto her wrist and stuck a dollar bill into the pocket of her shorts, just in case she decided to buy something to eat. She opened the front door.

"Mrow?" M.C. inquired.

"I'm going to the park," Kelly Ann told the cat. "But I'll be back soon. You stay here."

M.C. had no intention of being left behind. As Kelly Ann started down the street, he strolled along beside her, tail held high, head in the air.

"M.C., you silly thing," Kelly Ann said with

a grin. "Why don't you go home and take a nap in Samantha's house?"

All she got for an answer was an impatient flick of the crooked tail.

"All right," Kelly Ann surrendered. "But let's walk on Glendale. There are fewer cars."

Glendale Avenue was a back way to the park. It had never been paved. It was so full of ruts and bumps that not many people drove down it unless they had to.

Kelly Ann and M.C. had hardly turned into the street, however, when a green car passed them. Kelly Ann glanced at the driver—and she quickly looked again. It was Mrs. Barnett—and with her, almost certainly, was Mary Watson!

Kelly Ann had only met Mary Watson once, one afternoon when she and Hillary had gone to see her Persian kittens. But Mrs. Watson's hair was unmistakable. It was a shiny blue-black— "dye," Hillary pronounced—with a snow-white streak on one side. She always wore it piled elaborately on top of her head.

Maybe the women were on their way to drop off the ransom money! But why wasn't Hillary tailing them?

Kelly Ann began to run. "Surely M.C. will go home now," she thought. But she was wrong. The big gray cat loped easily along beside her.

Mrs. Barnett's car was pulled up next to the wooden railing at the edge of the park. She was still sitting behind the wheel. But Mrs. Watson was gone!

Kelly Ann looked frantically around. There she was! Mary Watson was quickly walking up one of the graveled paths that crisscrossed the park. In her hand was a purple soft-drink can.

Avoiding being seen by Mrs. Barnett, Kelly Ann raced up a narrow trail through some trees. Then she cut back onto the path. Mary Watson was right in front of her.

M.C. was enjoying the adventure—almost too much. He scrambled up the trunk of a tree after a squirrel, then plummeted down again, his eyes sparkling with mischief, the fur on his tail all puffed out.

"Calm down!" Kelly Ann hissed. "We don't want her to notice us."

But Mrs. Watson looked neither to the right nor left. She walked straight to a wire trash container near a line of benches. She placed the can carefully in the container. Then she walked away.

"That's it!" Kelly Ann said to herself. "The money must be in the soda can! I have to call Hillary!"

There were pay phones all over the park, one of them not more than thirty feet away. Kelly Ann dug into her pocket for change—and came up with the dollar bill.

Where was she going to get change? There

weren't many people in this part of the park at this time of day. Everyone was probably over at the baseball field. Kelly Ann saw an ice-cream man in the distance, selling popsicles to two kids. She ran over to him.

"Do you have change for a dollar?" she asked breathlessly. "I have to make a phone call."

He was tall and thin, with mild green eyes behind wire-rimmed glasses. He kept the ice cream in a contraption that looked like a big, insulated shoulder bag. On his belt was a changemaker.

"Sure," he said pleasantly, pushing back his white cap. He took Kelly Ann's dollar and handed her three quarters, two dimes, and a nickel from the changemaker.

"Thanks very much," Kelly Ann said. She sprinted to a pay phone.

"Listen!" Kelly Ann said when Hillary answered. "Your mother was here at the park! And Mrs. Watson! I think the ransom money's in a soda can in a trash container. You've got to get over here right away!"

"Where are you?" Hillary asked excitedly.

"Near the southern end of the park, off Glendale," Kelly Ann told her.

"I'll be right there. Don't take your eyes off that soda can!"

Kelly Ann hung up the phone and sidled

slowly toward the trash container. But she stopped about fifteen feet short of it and plopped down on a bench. She didn't want to seem too obvious, just in case anyone was watching.

Instead, she focused on M.C., who was pretending to stalk a blue jay. The bird was so large that M.C. wouldn't have known what to do with it if he *had* caught it. Soon he grew tired of the game. He walked over to Kelly Ann, hopped up on the bench beside her, and stretched out in the sun. His eyes were closed, and he purred his rattly purr of contentment.

It was very peaceful in the park. The ice-cream man called out, "Popsicles, Eskimo Pies." Kelly Ann could hear people cheering over at the baseball field. An old woman fed a bag of bread crumbs to a group of fluttering sparrows. A boy tried to fly a red kite.

Nothing happened. The soda can stayed where it was. Nobody went near it. Could Kelly Ann have been wrong? Maybe it was nothing more than an empty soda can.

"Don't be silly!" Kelly Ann said to herself. "Why would she bring it all the way into the park just to throw it out?"

Still, what if there was nothing in it? Kelly Ann moved to a bench a few feet closer to the trash can. M.C. followed. Kelly Ann observed the can out of the corner of her eye. It looked ordinary enough, purple, with "grape soda" written on the side.

The ice-cream man wasn't far away now. Maybe she should buy an Eskimo Pie—it would give her something to do. Kelly Ann dug into her pocket for fifty cents.

She started to say, "I'd like an Eskimo Pie," but the words hung in her throat. The ice-cream man had stopped near the trash container. Casually, he leaned over and reached down into it. His right hand closed around the soda can. He pulled it out and dropped it into the top of his insulated bag!

Chapter Twelve

Click! Without really thinking of the consequences, Kelly Ann had lifted the camera to eye level and taken a picture of the ice–cream man grabbing the purple soda can!

The man started at the sound of the camera shutter. His head jerked around. His eyes met Kelly Ann's, then traveled downward to rest on M.C. "That cat again!" he snarled. "I thought I'd seen the last of him on Elm Street!"

His eyes had hardened. No longer mild, they were dark green and hostile. "Give me that camera!" he said menacingly. He took a step toward Kelly Ann.

"Hang on, Kelly Ann!" a voice called out. "I'm coming!"

It was only Hillary, but the cat-napper didn't know that. He spun around to run. But somehow his legs became entangled with M.C. He hit the ground with a thud. The top of his insulated shoulder bag flew open. Out spilled Popsicles, Eskimo Pies—and the purple soda can!

Leaving it all behind, the man lurched to his feet and dashed into the trees. Kelly Ann was

not far behind him. He was a faster runner, but Kelly Ann was able to keep track of him by the jingling of his changemaker. And she knew the park much better than he did.

"He must be running toward his truck," she reasoned. There was only one parking lot in that direction. Kelly Ann took a chance—she tried a shortcut. She arrived at the parking lot just after the cat-napper did.

He jumped into the cab of a white panel truck. As he revved the motor, Kelly Ann noticed the license plate number reading MPV six-two-three-eight. And above the telltale digits, she saw that the back door of the truck was hanging open.

In a minute, the cat-napper would have made his escape. He didn't have Mrs. Watson's ransom money. But somewhere he had Farrah Fawcett, and probably several other kidnapped cats as well. Sergeant Thomas had told Mrs. Gill that the cat-napper would dump cats after he received his money, or worse. So they had to be found. And there was only one way to do that.

Kelly Ann took a deep breath. She darted to the back door of the truck and slipped inside. With any luck, the cat-napper hadn't seen her.

The white truck tore out of the parking lot and rounded the corner on two wheels, throwing Kelly Ann against one metal wall and then the other. At the back of the otherwise empty truck was a large ice chest, bolted to the floor. Kelly Ann crawled toward it and hung on for dear life. "Please, Hillary," she said to herself, "think of some way to get me out of this!"

Hillary had skidded her bike to a stop next to the pile of melting Popsicles and Eskimo Pies. She grabbed the purple soda can and peered into the slot in the top. The top would have to be cut off to get it out, but there was definitely a roll of bills in there.

M.C. reappeared from under a park bench, where he had taken cover. Neither the man in white nor Kelly Ann was anywhere in sight now. Hillary dropped her bike. Clutching the soda can, she set out after them, up the trail she had seen them take through the trees. But when she finally reached the parking lot, it was empty. The screech of tires farther down Tanner Road told her that the man had escaped. Kelly Ann must be with him!

Hillary found a pay phone and dialed the police emergency number. "Please," she said to the woman who answered, "I have to speak to Sergeant Thomas—it's urgent!

"Kelly Ann found the cat-napper in Garland Park," Hillary told the sergeant hurriedly. "And I have some of his ransom money. But the man has gotten away. I think he took Kelly Ann with him!"

"Did you see what he looked like?" Sergeant Thomas asked.

"Tall, and he was dressed all in white," Hillary said, "like an ice-cream vendor. It *had* to be the same man we saw six nights ago, and the same man who was driving the white truck that hit M.C. He left the parking lot at the south end of the park and drove down Tanner Road!"

"Don't worry, we'll find Kelly Ann," the sergeant promised her. "Just stay where you are. I'll send an officer to pick you up."

Hillary hung up the phone and just stood there. "I should be doing something," she said helplessly.

"Mrow," M.C. answered. He had followed her through the park.

Hillary picked up the gray cat and, for once, he didn't struggle. He reached out with a soft paw and touched her cheek.

At first Kelly Ann had tried to keep track of the turns the cat-napper made: two to the right after leaving the park, one to the left, another to the right. Soon, however, she was completely confused. She didn't know which direction they were going. And she was scared!

There was a rumble of traffic outside. They were slowing down. Finally the panel truck stopped. Kelly Ann could hear a jackhammer not far away. Had the cat-napper stopped at the traffic light on Main Street?

The jackhammer might be the men putting in a new sidewalk in front of the bank. Maybe she could slip out of the truck while it was stopped and find a policeman.

Kelly Ann rose to her feet from where she was crouched next to the ice chest. Suddenly the truck jumped forward! Kelly Ann staggered and fell against the chest. The heavy top came off and hit the wall with a clatter. If the cat-napper hadn't known he had an uninvited passenger, he certainly did now!

Kelly Ann was probably going to find out where the kidnapped cats were being held. But who was going to find *her*? Her only chance was to jump out of the truck as soon as it stopped again.

She scrambled back toward the door. The wheels were no longer moving over smooth blacktop. The road had gotten much rougher. The truck was slowing down. Then it braked to a stop with a screech!

Kelly Ann flung wide the door of the truck, ready to jump. She found herself face-to-face with the man in white!

He smiled at her grimly. "The nosy little photographer," he said. "Leaving so soon? I think you'd better come with me."

He grabbed Kelly Ann by the arm and started to drag her roughly out of the truck. "This is

a complication I didn't need!" he snarled, giving her a shake.

Suddenly a voice rang out loud and clear: "Turn the girl loose and step back fast! Put your hands up—we've got you covered!"

"Easy, easy," the cat-napper whined. "I'm not armed." He dropped Kelly Ann's arm and backed away with his hands in the air.

Kelly Ann poked her head cautiously out of the back of the truck. It was Officer Willis—and Sergeant Thomas!

Chapter Thirteen

"Willis, handcuff him and put him in the squad car," Sergeant Thomas directed. "And radio headquarters that we found Miss McCoy. Are you okay, Kelly Ann?" he asked, helping her down from the white truck.

"I'm fine," Kelly Ann said. "Just a little bit scared. I'm awfully glad to see *you*. I didn't think anyone was going to be able to find me."

"Your friend Hillary gave us a call, said you were headed down Tanner Road away from the park. One of the patrolmen picked up a white truck going through town in a hurry. Willis and I trailed you out here," the sergeant finished.

"Where are we?" Kelly Ann asked, looking around at three dilapidated buildings in the middle of trees and fields.

"This is the old Carolson farm," Sergeant Thomas answered. "It's been abandoned for years. It's far enough away from everything so that no one could hear any of the animals he might have stolen.

"Now, I'd better take a look in the house, just to make sure this guy was working alone," the sergeant told her.

He approached the tumbledown farmhouse warily, hand on revolver, and disappeared inside. But he was soon out again. "I think you may be able to help me," Sergeant Thomas said to Kelly Ann. "Come in and take a look at the cats."

Inside the old kitchen were six wire cages. And in five of them were beautiful cats.

"This is a Rex," Kelly Ann said, pointing to a slender white cat with short wavy hair. "It looks just like the picture in the cat book Hillary has."

The next two cats were Siamese. They talked to Kelly Ann in their harsh, plaintive voices.

"And this is Farrah Fawcett!" Kelly Ann exclaimed. "Mrs. Watson's cat. Thank goodness, she looks okay!"

The cream-colored Persian rolled over on her back and purred loudly when she heard her name called.

The fifth cat was gray striped, with short ears that actually folded forward. "I've never seen a picture of anything like this one," Kelly Ann said. "Isn't he cute?"

"We know who Farrah Fawcett belongs to," Sergeant Thomas said. "But how about taking pictures of the other four with that camera on your wrist? We'll have them developed this afternoon and print them in tomorrow's edition of the *Windsor Watchman*. That should make it much easier to locate their owners."

Kelly Ann snapped a photograph of each of the four cats. Then Sergeant Thomas took a picture of Kelly Ann standing next to the cages.

"That's it," he said. "End of the film."

The four cats, and the one with Kelly Ann, made five exposures. "But there were six exposures left," Kelly Ann murmured. Then she remembered what all of the excitement had made her forget. "I took a picture of the cat-napper picking up the ransom money," Kelly Ann told the sergeant.

"Great work!" Sergeant Thomas said. "I should hire you as an undercover officer."

"Don't forget M.C.," Kelly Ann added. "He got us started on all this."

There was a big reunion back at the police station. Hillary was there with Mrs. Watson's ransom money, and so was M.C. He was enjoying a visit with his old pals on the force.

Then the McCoys arrived straight from their baseball game. Mr. McCoy gave Kelly Ann a big hug and held her tight. "I couldn't worry before," he said, "because I didn't know about it. But now that I know about it, I intend to worry *plenty*."

Kelly Ann's photographs of the cat-napped cats were on the front page of the paper the next day, along with the picture she had taken of the phony ice-cream man clutching the soda can full of ransom money. Full credit was given to Kelly Ann McCoy as the photographer.

Sergeant Thomas called the girls at Hillary's house with some additional information about the cat-napper. "He's a drifter named Robert Grimes. We found an article in the farmhouse that he must have cut out of the *Windsor Watchman* a few weeks ago," the sergeant said. "It was about the upcoming cat show in the middle of September. He must have noticed the names of some of the exhibitors—like Mrs. Gill, Mrs. Watson, and the Garsons at the end of your street, Hillary. He probably figured they would be willing to pay a lot to get their valuable cats back and went to work.

"He slapped some white paint on his old truck, wore a white shirt and pants and a white hat. That way, people would notice the truck and uniform, not the man himself.

"He'd drive around in the truck in the daytime, casing the neighborhood. He kept popsicles and Eskimo Pies in an ice chest, just in case anyone asked to buy some ice cream.

"Then he'd come back at night and lure cats into the truck with catnip."

"M.C. must have stepped in some ice cream that had melted in the back of the truck," Hillary said. "That's why he and the Himalayan cat smelled like chocolate."

"I think it's pretty likely," the sergeant agreed. "One more thing—remember how M.C. tripped the cat-napper? Bits of catnip had lodged in the cuffs of Grimes's pants."

"And M.C. was just trying to get to it!" Hillary laughed. "He'll do anything for catnip."

Hillary hung up the phone. "That about wraps it up," she said to Kelly Ann. She lay back on her bed. There was a protesting squeak from M.C.

"Doesn't he look mysterious?" Hillary said. Mystery Cat was on his pillow with his feet in the air, his eyes narrowed to slits against the bright sunlight.

Chapter Fourteen

Two weeks later, school started. Kelly Ann and Hillary were both busy with new classes and lots of homework. But they had been specially invited to the final day of the Orchard County Cat Show.

Mary Watson had been very insistent when she had found the girls at Hillary's house. "It's next Saturday, and I want you to see Farrah Fawcett walk away with a blue ribbon. It's thanks to you two—"

"And M.C.," Hillary interjected.

"—and M.C.," Mary Watson agreed, "that I have Farrah at all. All those motherless kittens ...it would have been terrible."

"I'd like to go," Kelly Ann said.

"I would, too," said Hillary.

"Then I'll pick you up Saturday morning," Mrs. Watson told them. "We can have lunch at the Civic Center and you can see the judging and the final presentation of awards in the afternoon."

"It'll be fun," Kelly Ann said after Mrs. Watson had left.

"All those cats together aren't worth one of M.C." Hillary sniffed. "I'll bet not one of them ever solved a mystery in its life."

The girls had a good time at the show. "It's *Fabulous Felines* in the flesh," Hillary exclaimed.

"There's the white Rex we found at the farm," Kelly Ann told her. The side of his large cage was covered with blue and red ribbons.

"Hey, there's one of those flop-eared cats," Hillary said. "Scottish Fold," she read from the card attached to its cage. It had won something, too.

The girls watched the long-haired cats being powdered and brushed, the short-haired cats being oiled and groomed. Then the judges visited the winners in each breed to determine best of breed and best of show.

At last it was time for the presentation of the awards. A woman stepped onto the auditorium's stage and spoke into a microphone. "Before we announce the final awards for the Thirty-Ninth Annual Orchard County Cat Show," she said, "there is a very special award we would like to present."

Hillary nudged Kelly Ann. "Isn't that your mom over there, with the twins?" she whispered.

Kelly Ann nodded. "What would they be doing here?" she asked.

"To make the presentation," the woman

went on, "I'd like to call on last year's president of the Windsor Cat Breeders' Association, our own Mrs. Richard T. Gill."

Now it was Kelly Ann's turn to nudge Hillary, who glared at the stage.

The plump, gray-haired woman scurried out onstage and lowered the microphone a little. "Ahem," she said. "This is a new category of award for the Orchard County Cat Show, something we're calling the Life Achievement Award. It will be presented to that cat who in his or her life has made the most positive contribution to the feline community in Orchard County. This year's recipient, through his intelligence and courage, made it possible for at least six cats to appear here who otherwise might never have appeared again—here or anywhere else. One of them was my own Tupten Kanchenjunga. So I am especially proud to present the first Life Achievement Award to...M.C.—Mystery Cat! Will his two handlers, Kelly Ann McCoy and Hillary Barnett, please join me onstage?"

There was a big round of applause as Mary Watson propelled the astonished girls toward the front of the auditorium.

Then onto the stage marched Mr. Barnett and Mr. McCoy, carrying a huge cardboard box from which erupted unnerving growls and hisses. They put the box down on the floor and waited for their daughters to take over.

Hillary opened the box, and Kelly Ann lifted out a very cross M.C. "Don't embarrass us," she whispered to him.

Mrs. Gill picked up an enormous purple ribbon from a small table next to the microphone and presented it to Hillary. "For M.C.," she said, "with much gratitude from the Windsor Cat Breeders' Association."

"Thank you very much for all three of us," Hillary said graciously.

The auditorium rang with applause. Mrs. McCoy and the twins and Mrs. Barnett had seats right in front of the stage. They clapped the loudest.

"Do you think he'll remain a mystery cat, now that he's become a public figure?" Kelly Ann asked Hillary as they carried the gray tom offstage.

M.C. had an answer for that. He promptly disappeared for two days. And returned looking as mysterious as ever.

About the Author

Susan Saunders was born in San Antonio, Texas. After earning a B.A. from Barnard College in New York City, she began a career in publishing. She worked as an editor, writer, and designer for several major film companies and publishing houses.

Four years ago, Ms. Saunders left her position as editor to write full-time. She is the author of over twenty children's books, of which two were Junior Literary Guild selections, one a Book-of-the-Month Club Dragon Magic selection, and one a Notable Children's Trade Book chosen by the National Council for the Social Studies/Children's Book Council Joint Committee.

Ms. Saunders lives on Manhattan's Upper West Side where she cohabits with a Cairn terrier and three rambunctious cats.

About the Illustrator

Eileen Christelow is an author, artist, and professional photographer who lives in Marlboro, Vermont, with her husband, their daughter, and a cat named Maude.